Gabriel-Ernest
and Other Tales

Saki

Illustrated by Quentin Blake

ALMA CLASSICS LTD
Hogarth House
32-34 Paradise Road
Richmond
Surrey TW9 1SE
United Kingdom
www.almaclassics.com

This collection first published by Alma Classics Ltd in 2015
The texts reproduced in this volume are taken from the first editions of
the collections where they first appeared.

Illustrations © Quentin Blake, 2015

Extra Material © Alma Classics Ltd, 2015

Printed and bound by CPI Group (UK) Ltd, Croydon, CR0 4YY

ISBN: 978-1-84749-592-1

Contents

Gabriel-Ernest
and Other Tales

The Open Window

"MY AUNT WILL BE DOWN presently, Mr Nuttel," said a very self-possessed young lady of fifteen. "In the meantime you must try and put up with me."

Framton Nuttel endeavoured to say the correct something which should duly flatter the niece of the moment without unduly discounting the aunt that was to come. Privately he doubted more than ever whether these formal visits on a succession of total strangers would do much towards helping the nerve cure which he was supposed to be undergoing.

"I know how it will be," his sister had said when he was preparing to migrate to this rural retreat. "You will bury yourself down there and not speak to a living soul, and your nerves will be worse than ever from moping. I shall just give you letters of introduction to all the people I know there. Some of them, as far as I can remember, were quite nice."

Framton wondered whether Mrs Sappleton, the lady to whom he was presenting one of the letters of introduction, came into the "nice" division.

"Do you know many of the people round here?" asked the niece, when she judged that they had had sufficient silent communion.

"Hardly a soul," said Framton. "My sister was staying here, at the rectory, you know, some four years ago, and she gave me letters of introduction to some of the people here."

He made the last statement in a tone of distinct regret.

"Then you know practically nothing about my aunt?" pursued the self-possessed young lady.

"Only her name and address," admitted the caller. He was wondering whether Mrs Sappleton was in the married or widowed state. An undefinable something about the room seemed to suggest masculine habitation.

"Her great tragedy happened just three years ago," said the child. "That would be since your sister's time."

"Her tragedy?" asked Framton. Somehow in this restful country spot tragedies seemed out of place.

"You may wonder why we keep that window wide open on an October afternoon," said the niece, indicating a large French window that opened onto a lawn.

"It is quite warm for the time of the year," said Framton. "But has that window got anything to do with the tragedy?"

"Out through that window, three years ago to a day, her husband and her two young brothers went off for their day's shooting. They never came back. In crossing the moor to their favourite snipe-shooting ground they were all three engulfed in a treacherous piece of bog. It had been that dreadful wet summer, you know, and places that were safe in other years gave way suddenly without warning. Their bodies were never recovered. That was the dreadful part of it." Here the child's voice lost its self-possessed note and became falteringly human. "Poor aunt always thinks that they will come back some day – they and the little brown spaniel that was lost with them – and walk in at that window just as they used to do. That is why the window is kept open every evening till it is quite dusk. Poor dear aunt, she has often told me how they went out, her husband with his white waterproof coat over his arm, and Ronnie, her youngest brother, singing 'Bertie, why do you bound?' as he always did to tease her, because she said it got on her nerves. Do you know, sometimes on still, quiet evenings like this, I almost get a creepy feeling that they will all walk in through that window—"

She broke off with a little shudder. It was a relief to Framton when the aunt bustled into the room with a whirl of apologies for being late in making her appearance.

"I hope Vera has been amusing you?" she said.

"She has been very interesting," said Framton.

"I hope you don't mind the open window," said Mrs Sappleton briskly. "My husband and brothers will be home directly from shooting, and they always come in this way. They've been out for snipe in the marshes today, so they'll make a fine mess over my poor carpets. So like you menfolk, isn't it?"

She rattled on cheerfully about the shooting and the scarcity of birds, and the prospects for duck in the winter. To Framton, it was all purely horrible. He made a desperate but only partially successful effort to turn the talk onto a less ghastly topic: he was conscious that his hostess was giving him only a fragment of her attention, and her eyes were constantly straying past him to the open window and the lawn beyond. It was certainly an unfortunate coincidence that he should have paid his visit on this tragic anniversary.

"The doctors agree in ordering me complete rest, an absence of mental excitement and avoidance of anything in the nature of violent physical exercise," announced Framton, who laboured under the tolerably widespread delusion that total strangers and chance acquaintances are hungry for the least detail of one's ailments and infirmities, their cause and cure. "On the matter of diet they are not so much in agreement," he continued.

"No?" said Mrs Sappleton, in a voice which only replaced a yawn at the last moment. Then she suddenly brightened into alert attention – but not to what Framton was saying.

"Here they are at last!" she cried. "Just in time for tea, and don't they look as if they were muddy up to the eyes!"

Framton shivered slightly and turned towards the niece with a look intended to convey sympathetic comprehension. The child was staring out through the open window with dazed horror in her eyes. In a chill shock of nameless fear Framton swung round in his seat and looked in the same direction.

In the deepening twilight three figures were walking across the lawn towards the window; they all carried guns under their arms, and one of them was additionally burdened with a white coat hung over his shoulders. A tired brown spaniel kept close at their heels. Noiselessly they neared the house, and then a hoarse young voice chanted out of the dusk: "I said, Bertie, why do you bound?"

Framton grabbed wildly at his stick and hat; the hall door, the gravel drive and the front gate were dimly noted stages in his headlong retreat. A cyclist coming along the road had to run into the hedge to avoid an imminent collision.

"Here we are, my dear," said the bearer of the white mackintosh, coming in through the window. "Fairly muddy, but most of it's dry. Who was that who bolted out as we came up?"

"A most extraordinary man, a Mr Nuttel," said Mrs Sappleton. "Could only talk about his illnesses, and dashed off without a word of goodbye or apology when you arrived. One would think he had seen a ghost."

"I expect it was the spaniel," said the niece calmly. "He told me he had a horror of dogs. He was once hunted into a cemetery somewhere on the banks of the Ganges by a pack of pariah dogs, and had to spend the night in a newly dug grave with the creatures snarling and grinning and foaming just above him. Enough to make anyone lose their nerve."

Romance at short notice was her speciality.

The Boar-Pig

"THERE IS A BACK WAY onto the lawn," said Mrs Philidore Stossen to her daughter, "through a small grass paddock and then through a walled fruit garden full of gooseberry bushes. I went all over the place last year when the family were away. There is a door that opens from the fruit garden into a shrub- bery, and once we emerge from there we can mingle with the guests as if we had come in by the ordinary way. It's much safer than going in by the front entrance and running the risk of coming bang up against the hostess – that would be so awkward when she doesn't happen to have invited us."

"Isn't it a lot of trouble to take for getting admittance to a garden party?"

"To a garden party, yes; to *the* garden party of the season, certainly not. Everyone of any consequence in the county, with the exception of ourselves, has been asked to meet the Princess, and it would be far more troublesome to invent explanations as to why

we weren't there than to get in by a roundabout way. I stopped Mrs Cuvering in the road yesterday and talked very pointedly about the Princess. If she didn't choose to take the hint and send me an invitation it's not my fault, is it? Here we are: we just cut across the grass and through that little gate into the garden."

Mrs Stossen and her daughter, suitably arrayed for a county garden party function with an infusion of *Almanach de Gotha*, sailed through the narrow grass paddock and the ensuing gooseberry garden with the air of state barges making an unofficial progress along a rural trout stream. There was a certain amount of furtive haste mingled with the stateliness of their advance as though hostile searchlights might be turned on them at any moment – and, as a matter of fact, they were not unobserved. Matilda Cuvering, with the alert eyes of thirteen years old and the added advantage of an exalted position in the branches of a medlar tree, had enjoyed a good view of the Stossen flanking movement and had foreseen exactly where it would break down in execution.

"They'll find the door locked, and they'll jolly well have to go back the way they came," she remarked to herself. "Serves them right for not coming in by the proper entrance. What a pity Tarquin Superbus isn't loose in the paddock. After all, as everyone else is enjoying themselves, I don't see why Tarquin shouldn't have an afternoon out."

Matilda was of an age when thought is action: she slid down from the branches of the medlar tree, and when she clambered back again, Tarquin, the huge white Yorkshire boar-pig, had exchanged the narrow limits of his sty for the wider range of the grass paddock. The discomfited Stossen expedition, returning in recriminatory but otherwise orderly retreat from the unyielding obstacle of the locked door, came to a sudden halt at the gate dividing the paddock from the gooseberry garden.

"What a villainous-looking animal," exclaimed Mrs Stossen. "It wasn't there when we came in."

"It's there now, anyhow," said her daughter. "What on earth are we to do? I wish we had never come."

The boar-pig had drawn nearer to the gate for a closer inspection of the human intruders, and stood champing his jaws and blinking his small red eyes in a manner

that was doubtless intended to be disconcerting, and as far as the Stossens were concerned, thoroughly achieved that result.

"Shoo! Hish! Hish! Shoo!" cried the ladies in chorus.

"If they think they're going to drive him away by reciting lists of the kings of Israel and Judah they're laying themselves out for disappointment," observed Matilda from her seat in the medlar tree. As she made the observation aloud, Mrs Stossen became for the first time aware of her presence. A moment or two earlier she would have been anything but pleased at the discovery that the garden was not as deserted as it looked, but now she hailed the fact of the child's presence on the scene with absolute relief.

"Little girl, can you find someone to drive away—" she began hopefully.

"*Comment? Comprends pas*," was the response.

"Oh, are you French? *Êtes vous française?*"

"*Pas de tous. Suis anglaise.*"

"Then why not talk English? I want to know if—"

"*Permettez-moi expliquer.* You see, I'm rather under a cloud," said Matilda. "I'm staying with my aunt, and I was told I must behave particularly well today, as lots of people were coming for a garden party, and I was told to imitate Claude – that's my young cousin, who never does anything wrong except by accident, and then is always apologetic about it. It seems they thought I ate too much raspberry trifle at lunch, and they said Claude never eats too much raspberry trifle. Well, Claude always goes to sleep for half an hour after lunch, because he's told to, and I waited till he was asleep, and tied his hands and started forcible feeding with a whole bucketful of raspberry trifle that they were keeping for the garden party. Lots of it went onto his sailor suit and some of it onto the bed, but a good deal went down Claude's throat, and they can't say again that he has never been known to eat too much raspberry trifle. That is why I am not allowed to go to the party, and as an additional punishment I must speak French all the afternoon. I've had to tell you all this in English, as there were words like 'forcible feeding' that I didn't know the French for – of course I could have invented them, but if I had said *nourriture obligatoire* you wouldn't have had the least idea what I was talking about. *Mais maintenant, nous parlons français.*"

"Oh, very well, *très bien,*" said Mrs Stossen reluctantly: in moments of flurry such French as she knew was not under very good control. "*Là, à l'autre côté de la porte, est un cochon—*"

"*Un cochon? Ah, le petit charmant!*" exclaimed Matilda with enthusiasm.

"*Mais non, pas du tout petit, et pas du tout charmant: un bête féroce—*"

"*Une bête*," corrected Matilda. "A pig is masculine as long as you call it a pig, but if you lose your temper with it and call it a ferocious beast, it becomes one of us at once. French is a dreadfully unsexing language."

"For Goodness' sake, let us talk English then," said Mrs Stossen. "Is there any way out of this garden except through the paddock where the pig is?"

"I always go over the wall, by way of the plum tree," said Matilda.

"Dressed as we are we could hardly do that," said Mrs Stossen. It was difficult to imagine her doing it in any costume.

"Do you think you could go and get someone who would drive the pig away?" asked Miss Stossen.

"I promised my aunt I would stay here till five o'clock: it's not four yet."

"I am sure, under the circumstances, your aunt would permit—"

"My conscience would not permit," said Matilda with cold dignity.

"We can't stay here till five o'clock," exclaimed Mrs Stossen with growing exasperation.

"Shall I recite to you to make the time pass quicker?" asked Matilda obligingly. "'Belinda, the little Breadwinner' is considered my best piece – or, perhaps, it ought to be something in French. Henri Quatre's address to his soldiers is the only thing I really know in that language."

"If you will go and fetch someone to drive that animal away I will give you something to buy yourself a nice present," said Mrs Stossen.

Matilda came several inches lower down the medlar tree.

"That is the most practical suggestion you have made yet for getting out of the garden," she remarked cheerfully. "Claude and I are collecting money for the Children's Fresh Air Fund, and we are seeing which of us can collect the biggest sum."

"I shall be very glad to contribute half a crown, very glad indeed," said Mrs Stossen, digging that coin out of the depths of a receptacle which formed a detached outwork of her toilet.

"Claude is a long way ahead of me at present," continued Matilda, taking no notice of the suggested

offering. "You see, he's only eleven, and has golden hair, and those are enormous advantages when you're on the collecting job. Only the other day a Russian lady gave him ten shillings. Russians understand the art of giving far better than we do. I expect Claude will net quite twenty-five shillings this afternoon: he'll have the field to himself, and he'll be able to do the pale, fragile, not-long-for-this-world business to perfection after his raspberry-trifle experience. Yes, he'll be *quite* two pounds ahead of me by now."

With much probing and plucking and many regretful murmurs, the beleaguered ladies managed to produce seven-and-sixpence between them.

"I am afraid this is all we've got," said Mrs Stossen.

Matilda showed no sign of coming down either to the earth or to their figure.

"I could not do violence to my conscience for anything less than ten shillings," she announced stiffly.

Mother and daughter muttered certain remarks under their breath, in which the word "beast" was prominent, and probably had no reference to Tarquin.

"I find I *have* got another half-crown," said Mrs Stossen in a shaking voice. "Here you are. Now please fetch someone quickly."

Matilda slipped down from the tree, took possession of the donation and proceeded to pick up a handful of overripe medlars from the grass at her feet. Then she climbed over the gate and addressed herself affectionately to the boar-pig.

"Come, Tarquin, dear old boy – you know you can't resist medlars when they're rotten and squashy."

Tarquin couldn't. By dint of throwing the fruit in front of him at judicious intervals, Matilda decoyed him back to his sty, while the delivered captives hurried across the paddock.

"Well, I never! The little minx!" exclaimed Mrs Stossen when she was safely on the high road. "The animal wasn't savage at all, and as for the ten shillings, I don't believe the Fresh Air Fund will see a penny of it!"

There she was unwarrantably harsh in her judgement. If you examine the books of the fund, you will find the acknowledgement: "Collected by Miss Matilda Cuvering, 2s. 6d."

The Chaplet

A STRANGE STILLNESS HUNG over the restaurant: it was one of those rare moments when the orchestra was not discoursing the strains of the 'Ice Cream Sailor' waltz.

"Did I ever tell you," asked Clovis of his friend, "the tragedy of music at mealtimes?

"It was a gala evening at the Grand Sybaris Hotel, and a special dinner was being served in the Amethyst dining hall. The Amethyst dining hall had almost a European reputation, especially with that section of Europe which is historically identified with the Jordan Valley. Its cooking was beyond reproach, and its orchestra was sufficiently highly salaried to be above criticism. Thither came in shoals the intensely musical and the almost intensely musical, who are very many, and in still greater numbers the merely musical, who know how Tchaikovsky's name is pronounced and can recognize several of Chopin's Nocturnes if you give them due warning: these eat in the nervous, detached manner of roebuck feeding in the open, and keep anxious ears cocked towards the orchestra for the first hint of a recognizable melody.

"'Ah, yes, *Pagliacci*,' they murmur, as the opening strains follow hot upon the soup, and if no contradiction is forthcoming from any better-informed quarter, they break forth into subdued humming by way of supplementing the efforts of the musicians. Sometimes the melody starts on level terms with the soup, in which case the banqueters contrive somehow to hum between the spoonfuls; the facial expression of enthusiasts who are punctuating *potage Saint-Germain* with *Pagliacci* is not beautiful, but it should be seen by those who are bent on observing all sides of life. One cannot discount the unpleasant things of this world merely by looking the other way.

"In addition to the aforementioned types, the restaurant was patronized by a fair sprinkling of the absolutely non-musical: their presence in the dining hall could only be explained on the supposition that they had come there to dine.

"The earlier stages of the dinner had worn off. The wine lists had been consulted, by some with the blank embarrassment of a schoolboy suddenly called on to locate a minor prophet in the tangled hinterland of the Old Testament, by others with the severe scrutiny which suggests that they have visited most of the higher-priced wines in their own homes and probed their family weaknesses. The diners who chose their wine in the latter fashion always gave their orders in a penetrating voice, with a plentiful garnishing of stage directions. By insisting on having your bottle pointing to the north when the cork is being drawn, and calling the waiter Max, you may induce an impression on your guests which hours of laboured boasting might be powerless to achieve. For this purpose, however, the guests must be chosen as carefully as the wine.

"Standing aside from the revellers in the shadow of a massive pillar was an interested spectator who was assuredly of the feast, and yet not in it. Monsieur Aristide Saucourt was the *chef* of the Grand Sybaris Hotel, and if he had an equal in his profession, he had never acknowledged the fact. In his own domain he was a potentate, hedged around with the cold brutality that genius expects rather than excuses in her children; he

31

never forgave, and those who served him were careful that there should be little to forgive. In the outer world, the world which devoured his creations, he was an influence – how profound or how shallow an influence he never attempted to guess. It is the penalty and the safeguard of genius that it computes itself by troy weight in a world that measures by vulgar hundredweights.

"Once in a way the great man would be seized with a desire to watch the effect of his master efforts, just as the guiding brain of Krupp's might wish at a supreme moment to intrude into the firing line of an artillery duel. And such an occasion was the present. For the first time in the history of the Grand Sybaris Hotel, he was presenting to its guests the dish which he had brought to that pitch of perfection which almost amounts to scandal. Canetons à la mode d'Amblève. In thin gilt lettering on the creamy white of the menu, how little those words conveyed to the bulk of the imperfectly educated diners! And yet how much specialized effort had been lavished, how much carefully treasured lore had been ungarnered, before those six words could be written! In the Department of Deux-Sèvres, ducklings had lived peculiar and beautiful lives and died in the odour of satiety to furnish the main theme of the dish; *champignons*, which even a purist for Saxon English would have hesitated to address as mushrooms, had contributed their languorous atrophied bodies to the garnishing, and a sauce devised in the twilight reign of the Fifteenth Louis had been summoned back from the imperishable past to take its part in the wonderful confection. Thus far had human effort laboured to achieve the desired result: the rest had been left to human genius – the genius of Aristide Saucourt.

"And now the moment had arrived for the serving of the great dish, the dish which world-weary Grand Dukes and market-obsessed money magnates counted among their happiest memories. And at the same moment something else happened. The leader of the highly salaried orchestra placed his violin caressingly against his chin, lowered his eyelids and floated into a sea of melody.

"'Hark!' said most of the diners, 'he is playing "The Chaplet."'"

"They knew it was 'The Chaplet' because they had heard it played at luncheon and afternoon tea, and at supper the night before, and had not had time to forget.

"'Yes, he is playing "The Chaplet",' they reassured one another. The general voice was unanimous on the subject. The orchestra had already played it eleven times that day, four times by desire and seven times from force of habit, but the familiar strains were greeted with the rapture due to a revelation. A murmur of much humming rose from half the tables in the room, and some of the more overwrought listeners laid down knife and fork in order to be able to burst in with loud clappings at the earliest permissible moment.

"And the Canetons à la mode d'Amblève? In stupefied, sickened wonder, Aristide watched them grow cold in total neglect, or suffer the almost worse indignity of perfunctory pecking and listless munching while the banqueters lavished their approval and applause on the

music-makers. Calves' liver and bacon, with parsley sauce, could hardly have figured more ignominiously in the evening's entertainment. And while the master of culinary art leant back against the sheltering pillar, choking with a horrible brain-searing rage that could find no outlet for its agony, the orchestra leader was bowing his acknowledgements of the hand-clappings that rose in a storm around him. Turning to his colleagues, he nodded the signal for an encore. But before the violin had been lifted anew into position, there came from the shadow of the pillar an explosive negative.

"'Noh! Noh! You do not play thot again!'

"The musician turned in furious astonishment. Had he taken warning from the look in the other man's eyes, he might have acted differently. But the admiring plaudits were ringing in his ears, and he snarled out sharply: 'That is for me to decide.'

"'Noh! You play thot never again,' shouted the *chef*, and the next moment he had flung himself violently upon the loathed being who had supplanted him in the world's esteem. A large metal tureen, filled to the brim with steaming soup, had just been placed on a side table in readiness for a late party of diners; before the waiting staff or the guests had time to realize what was happening, Aristide had dragged his struggling victim up to the table and plunged his head deep down into the almost boiling contents of the tureen. At the further end of the room, the diners were still spasmodically applauding in view of an encore.

"Whether the leader of the orchestra died from drowning by soup or from the shock to his professional vanity, or was scalded to death, the doctors were never wholly able to agree. Monsieur Aristide Saucourt, who now lives in complete retirement, always inclined to the drowning theory."

The Lumber Room

T HE CHILDREN WERE to be driven, as a special treat, to the sands at Jagborough. Nicholas was not to be of the party: he was in disgrace. Only that morning he had refused to eat his wholesome bread-and-milk on the seemingly frivolous ground that there was a frog in it. Older and wiser and better people had

told him that there could not possibly be a frog in his bread-and-milk and that he was not to talk nonsense; he continued, nevertheless, to talk what seemed the veriest nonsense, and described with much detail the colouration and markings of the alleged frog. The dramatic part of the incident was that there really was a frog in Nicholas's basin of bread-and-milk: he had put it there himself, so he felt entitled to know something about it. The sin of taking a frog from the garden and putting it into a bowl of wholesome bread-and-milk was enlarged on at great length, but the fact that stood out clearest in the whole affair, as it presented itself to the mind of Nicholas, was that the older, wiser and better people had been proved to be profoundly in error in matters about which they had expressed the utmost assurance.

"You said there couldn't possibly be a frog in my bread-and-milk; there *was* a frog in my bread-and-milk," he repeated, with the insistence of a skilled tactician who does not intend to shift from favourable ground.

So his boy-cousin and girl-cousin and his quite uninteresting younger brother were to be taken to Jagborough

Sands that afternoon and he was to stay at home. His cousins' aunt, who insisted, by an unwarranted stretch of imagination, in styling herself his aunt also, had hastily invented the Jagborough expedition in order to impress on Nicholas the delights that he had justly forfeited by his disgraceful conduct at the breakfast table. It was her habit, whenever one of the children fell from grace, to improvise something of a festival nature from which the offender would be rigorously debarred; if all the children sinned collectively, they were suddenly informed of a circus in a neighbouring town, a circus of unrivalled merit and uncounted elephants – to which, but for their depravity, they would have been taken that very day.

A few decent tears were looked for on the part of Nicholas when the moment for the departure of the expedition arrived. As a matter of fact, however, all the crying was done by his girl-cousin, who scraped her knee rather painfully against the step of the carriage as she was scrambling in.

"How she did howl," said Nicholas cheerfully, as the party drove off without any of the elation of high spirits that should have characterized it.

"She'll soon get over that," said the *soi-disant* aunt. "It will be a glorious afternoon for racing about over those beautiful sands. How they will enjoy themselves!"

"Bobby won't enjoy himself much, and he won't race much either," said Nicholas with a grim chuckle. "His boots are hurting him. They're too tight."

"Why didn't he tell me they were hurting?" asked the aunt with some asperity.

"He told you twice, but you weren't listening. You often don't listen when we tell you important things."

"You are not to go into the gooseberry garden," said the aunt, changing the subject.

"Why not?" demanded Nicholas.

"Because you are in disgrace," said the aunt loftily.

Nicholas did not admit the flawlessness of the reasoning: he felt perfectly capable of being in disgrace and in a gooseberry garden at the same moment. His face took on an expression of considerable obstinacy. It was clear to his aunt that he was determined to get into the gooseberry garden "only," as she remarked to herself, "because I have told him he is not to."

44

Now, the gooseberry garden had two doors by which it might be entered, and once a small person like Nicholas could slip in there he could effectually disappear from view amid the masking growth of artichokes, raspberry canes and fruit bushes. The aunt had many other things to do that afternoon, but she spent an hour or two in trivial gardening operations among flower beds and shrubberies, whence she could keep a watchful eye on the two doors that led to the forbidden paradise. She was a woman of few ideas, with immense powers of concentration.

Nicholas made one or two sorties into the front garden, wriggling his way with obvious stealth of purpose towards one or other of the doors, but never able for a moment to evade the aunt's watchful eye. As a matter of fact, he had no intention of trying to get into the gooseberry garden, but it was extremely convenient for him that his aunt should believe that he had: it was a belief that would keep her on self-imposed sentry duty for the greater part of the after-noon. Having thoroughly confirmed and fortified her suspicions, Nicholas slipped back into the house and rapidly put into execution a plan of action that had long germinated in his brain. By standing on a chair in the library, one could reach a shelf on which reposed a fat, important-looking key. The key was as important as it looked: it was the instrument which kept the mysteries of the lumber room secure from unauthorized intrusion, which opened a way only for aunts and suchlike privileged persons. Nicholas had not much experience of the art of fitting keys into keyholes and turning locks, but for some days past he had practised with the key of the schoolroom door: he did not believe in trusting too much to luck and accident. The key turned stiffly in the lock, but it turned. The door opened, and Nicholas was in an unknown land, compared with which the gooseberry garden was a stale delight, a mere material pleasure.

Often and often Nicholas had pictured to himself what the lumber room might be like, that region that was so carefully sealed from youthful eyes and concerning which no questions were ever answered. It came up to his expectations. In the first place it was large and dimly lit, one high window opening onto the forbidden

garden being its only source of illumination. In the second place it was a storehouse of unimagined treasures. The aunt-by-assertion was one of those people who think that things spoil by use and consign them to dust and damp by way of preserving them. Such parts of the house as Nicholas knew best were rather bare and cheerless, but here there were wonderful things for the eye to feast on. First and foremost there was a piece of framed tapestry that was evidently meant to be a fire screen. To Nicholas it was a living, breathing story; he sat down on a roll of Indian hangings, glowing in wonderful colours beneath a layer of dust, and took in all the details of the tapestry picture. A man, dressed in the hunting costume of some remote period, had just transfixed a stag with an arrow – it could not have been a difficult shot, because the stag was only one or two paces away from him; in the thickly growing vegetation that the picture suggested it would not have been difficult to creep up to a feeding stag, and the two spotted dogs that were springing forward to join in the chase had evidently been trained to keep to heel till the arrow was discharged. That part of the picture was simple, if interesting, but did the huntsman see what Nicholas saw – that four galloping wolves were coming in his direction through the wood? There might be more than four of them hidden behind the trees, and in any case would the man and his dogs be able to cope with the four wolves if they made an attack? The man had only two arrows left in his quiver, and he might miss with one or both of them – all one knew about his skill in shooting was that he could hit a large stag at a ridiculously short range. Nicholas sat for many golden minutes revolving the possibilities of the scene; he was inclined to think that there were more than four wolves and that the man and his dogs were in a tight corner.

But there were other objects of delight and interest claiming his instant attention: there were quaint, twisted candlesticks in the shape of snakes, and a teapot fashioned like a china duck, out of whose open beak the tea was supposed to come. How dull and shapeless the nursery teapot seemed in comparison! And there was a carved sandal-wood box packed tight with aromatic cotton wool, and between the layers of cotton wool were little brass figures, hump-necked bulls and peacocks and goblins, delightful to see and to handle. Less promising in appearance was a large square book with plain black covers: Nicholas peeped into it and, behold, it was full of coloured pictures of birds. And such birds! In the garden, and in the lanes when he went for a walk, Nicholas came across a few birds, of

which the largest were an occasional magpie or wood pigeon; here were herons and bustards, kites, toucans, tiger-bitterns, brush turkeys, ibises, golden pheasants, a whole portrait gallery of undreamed-of creatures. And as he was admiring the colouring of the mandarin duck and assigning a life history to it, the voice of his aunt in shrill vociferation of his name came from the gooseberry garden without. She had grown suspicious at his long disappearance and had leapt to the conclusion that he had climbed over the wall behind the sheltering screen of the lilac bushes; she was now engaged in energetic and rather hopeless search for him among the artichokes and raspberry canes.

"Nicholas, Nicholas!" she screamed, "you are to come out of this at once. It's no use trying to hide there: I can see you all the time."

It was probably the first time for twenty years that anyone had smiled in that lumber room.

Presently the angry repetitions of Nicholas's name gave way to a shriek, and a cry for somebody to come quickly. Nicholas shut the book, restored it carefully to its place in a corner and shook some dust from a neighbouring pile of newspapers over it. Then he crept from the room, locked the door and replaced the key exactly where he had found it. His aunt was still calling his name when he sauntered into the front garden.

"Who's calling?" he asked.

"Me," came the answer from the other side of the wall. "Didn't you hear me? I've been looking for you in the gooseberry garden, and I've slipped into the rainwater tank. Luckily there's no water in it, but the sides are slippery and I can't get out. Fetch the little ladder from under the cherry tree—"

"I was told I wasn't to go into the gooseberry garden," said Nicholas promptly.

"I told you not to, and now I tell you that you may," came the voice from the rainwater tank, rather impatiently.

"Your voice doesn't sound like Aunt's," objected Nicholas. "You may be the Evil One tempting me to be disobedient. Aunt often tells me that the Evil One tempts me and that I always yield. This time I'm not going to yield."

"Don't talk nonsense," said the prisoner in the tank. "Go and fetch the ladder."

"Will there be strawberry jam for tea?" asked Nicholas innocently.

"Certainly there will be," said the aunt, privately resolving that Nicholas should have none of it.

"Now I know that you are the Evil One and not Aunt," shouted Nicholas gleefully. "When we asked aunt for strawberry jam yesterday, she said there wasn't any. I know there are four jars of it in the store cupboard, because I looked, and of course you know it's there, but *she* doesn't, because she said there wasn't any. Oh, Devil, you *have* sold yourself!"

There was an unusual sense of luxury in being able to talk to an aunt as though one was talking to the Evil One, but Nicholas knew, with childish discernment, that such luxuries were not to be overindulged in. He walked noisily away, and it was a kitchen maid, in search of parsley, who eventually rescued the aunt from the rainwater tank.

Tea that evening was partaken of in a fearsome silence. The tide had been at its highest when the children had arrived at Jagborough Cove, so there had been no sands to play on – a circumstance that the aunt had overlooked in the haste of organizing her punitive expedition. The tightness of Bobby's boots had had disastrous effect on his temper the whole of the afternoon, and altogether the children could not have been said to have enjoyed themselves. The aunt maintained the frozen muteness of one who has suffered undignified and unmerited detention in a rainwater tank for thirty-five minutes. As for Nicholas, he too was silent, in the absorption of one who has much to think about: it was just possible, he considered, that the huntsman would escape with his hounds while the wolves feasted on the stricken stag.

The Schartz-Metterklume
Method

L ADY CARLOTTA STEPPED out onto the platform of the small wayside station and took a turn or two up and down its uninteresting length, to kill time till the train should be pleased to proceed on its way. Then, in the roadway beyond, she saw a horse struggling with a more than ample load, and a carter of the sort that seems to bear a sullen hatred against the animal that helps him to earn a living. Lady Carlotta promptly betook her to the roadway and put rather a different complexion on the struggle. Certain of her acquaintances were wont to give her plentiful admonition as to the undesirability of interfering on behalf of a distressed animal, such interference being "none of her business". Only once had she put the doctrine of non-interference into practice, when one of its most eloquent exponents had been besieged for nearly three hours in a small and extremely uncomfortable may tree by an angry boar-pig, while Lady Carlotta, on the other side of the fence, had proceeded with the watercolour sketch she was engaged on and refused to interfere between the boar and his prisoner. It is to be feared that she lost the friendship of the ultimately rescued lady. On this occasion she merely lost the train, which gave way to the first sign of impatience it had shown throughout the journey and steamed off without her. She bore the desertion with philosophical indifference: her friends and relations were thoroughly well used to the fact of her luggage arriving without her. She wired a vague, non-committal message to her destination to say that she was coming on "by another train". Before she had time to think what her next move might be, she was confronted by an imposingly attired lady, who seemed to be taking a prolonged mental inventory of her clothes and looks.

"You must be Miss Hope, the governess I've come to meet," said the apparition, in a tone that admitted of very little argument.

"Very well, if I must I must," said Lady Carlotta to herself with dangerous meekness.

"I am Mrs Quabarl," continued the lady. "And where, pray, is your luggage?"

"It's gone astray," said the alleged governess, falling in with the excellent rule of life that the absent are always to blame: the luggage had, in point of fact, behaved with perfect correctitude. "I've just telegraphed about it," she added, with a nearer approach to truth.

"How provoking," said Mrs Quabarl. "These railway companies are so careless. However, my maid can lend you things for the night," and she led the way to her car.

During the drive to the Quabarl mansion, Lady Carlotta was impressively introduced to the nature of the charge that had been thrust upon her: she learned that Claude and Wilfrid were delicate, sensitive young people, that Irene had the artistic temperament highly developed, and that Viola was something or other else of a mould equally commonplace among children of that class and type in the twentieth century.

"I wish them not only to be *taught*," said Mrs Quabarl, "but *interested* in what they learn. In their history lessons, for instance, you must try to make them feel that they are being introduced to the life stories of men and women who really lived, not merely committing a mass of names and dates to memory. French, of

course, I shall expect you to talk at mealtimes several days in the week."

"I shall talk French four days of the week and Russian in the remaining three."

"Russian? My dear Miss Hope, no one in the house speaks or understands Russian."

"That will not embarrass me in the least," said Lady Carlotta coldly.

Mrs Quabarl, to use a colloquial expression, was knocked off her perch. She was one of those imperfectly self-assured individuals who are magnificent and autocratic as long as they are not seriously opposed. The least show of unexpected resistance goes a long way towards rendering them cowed and apologetic. When the new governess failed to express wondering admiration of the large, newly purchased and expensive car, and lightly alluded to the superior advantages of one or two makes which had just been put on the market, the discomfiture of her patroness became almost abject. Her feelings were those which might have animated a general of ancient warfaring days on beholding his heaviest battle elephant ignominiously driven off the field by slingers and javelin throwers.

At dinner that evening, although reinforced by her husband, who usually duplicated her opinions and lent her moral support generally, Mrs Quabarl regained none of her lost ground. The governess not only helped herself well and truly to wine, but held forth with considerable show of critical knowledge on various vintage matters, concerning which the Quabarls were in no wise able to pose as authorities. Previous governesses had limited their conversation on the wine topic to a respectful and doubtless sincere expression of a preference for water. When this one went as far as to recommend a wine firm in whose hands you could not go very far wrong, Mrs Quabarl thought it time to turn the conversation into more usual channels.

"We got very satisfactory references about you from Canon Teep," she observed, "a very estimable man, I should think."

"Drinks like a fish and beats his wife – otherwise a very lovable character," said the governess imperturbably.

"My *dear* Miss Hope! I trust you are exaggerating," exclaimed the Quabarls in unison.

"One must in justice admit that there is some provocation," continued the romancer. "Mrs Teep is quite the most irritating bridge player that I have ever sat down with: her leads and declarations would condone a certain amount of brutality in her partner, but to souse her with the contents of the only soda-water syphon in the house on a Sunday afternoon, when one couldn't get another, argues an indifference to the comfort of others which I cannot altogether overlook. You may think me hasty in my judgements, but it was practically on account of the syphon incident that I left."

"We will talk of this some other time," said Mrs Quabarl hastily.

"I shall never allude to it again," said the governess with decision.

Mr Quabarl made a welcome diversion by asking what studies the new instructress proposed to inaugurate on the morrow.

"History to begin with," she informed him.

"Ah, history," he observed sagely. "Now, in teaching them history you must take care to interest them in what they learn. You must make them feel that they are being introduced to the life stories of men and women who really lived—"

"I've told her all that," interposed Mrs Quabarl.

"I teach history on the Schartz-Metterklume method," said the governess loftily.

"Ah, yes," said her listeners, thinking it expedient to assume an acquaintance at least with the name.

"What are you children doing out here?" demanded Mrs Quabarl the next morning, on finding Irene sitting rather glumly at the head of the stairs, while her sister was perched in an attitude of depressed discomfort on the window seat behind her, with a wolfskin rug almost covering her.

"We are having a history lesson," came the unexpected reply. "I am supposed to be Rome, and Viola up there is the she-wolf – not a real wolf, but the figure of one that the Romans used to set store by... I forget why. Claude and Wilfrid have gone to fetch the shabby women."

"The shabby women?"

"Yes, they've got to carry them off. They didn't want to, but Miss Hope got one of father's fives-bats and said she'd give them a number-nine spanking if they didn't, so they've gone to do it."

A loud, angry screaming from the direction of the lawn drew Mrs Quabarl thither in hot haste, fearful lest the threatened castigation might even now be in process of infliction. The outcry, however, came principally from the two small daughters of the lodge-keeper, who were being hauled and pushed towards the house by the panting and dishevelled Claude and Wilfrid, whose task was rendered even more arduous by the incessant, if not very effectual, attacks of the captured maidens' small brother. The governess, fives-bat in hand, sat negligently on the stone balustrade, presiding over the scene with the cold impartiality of a Goddess of Battles. A furious and repeated chorus of "I'll tell muvver" rose from the lodge-children, but the lodge-mother, who was hard of hearing, was for the moment immersed in the preoccupation of her washtub. After an apprehensive glance in the direction of the lodge (the good woman was gifted with the highly militant temper which is sometimes the privilege of deafness), Mrs Quabarl flew indignantly to the rescue of the struggling captives.

"Wilfrid! Claude! Let those children go at once. Miss Hope, what on earth is the meaning of this scene?"

"Early Roman history – the Sabine women, don't you know? It's the Schartz-Metterklume method to make children understand history by acting it themselves: fixes it in their memory, you know. Of course if, thanks to your interference, your boys go through life thinking that the Sabine women ultimately escaped, I really cannot be held responsible."

"You may be very clever and modern, Miss Hope," said Mrs Quabarl firmly, "but I should like you to leave here by the next train. Your luggage will be sent after you as soon as it arrives."

"I'm not certain exactly where I shall be for the next few days," said the dismissed instructress of youth. "You might keep my luggage till I wire my address. There are only a couple of trunks and some golf clubs and a leopard cub."

"A leopard cub!" gasped Mrs Quabarl. Even in her departure this extraordinary person seemed destined to leave a trail of embarrassment behind her.

"Well, it's rather left off being a cub: it's more than half-grown, you know. A fowl every day and a rabbit on Sundays is what it usually gets. Raw beef makes it too excitable. Don't trouble about getting the car for me, I'm rather inclined for a walk."

And Lady Carlotta strode out of the Quabarl horizon.

The advent of the genuine Miss Hope, who had made a mistake as to the day on which she was due to arrive, caused a turmoil which that good lady was quite unused to inspiring. Obviously the Quabarl family had been woefully befooled, but a certain amount of relief came with the knowledge.

"How tiresome for you, dear Carlotta," said her hostess, when the overdue guest ultimately arrived. "How very tiresome losing your train and having to stop overnight in a strange place."

"Oh, dear, no," said Lady Carlotta, "not at all tiresome – for me."

Gabriel-Ernest

"THERE IS A WILD BEAST in your woods," said the artist Cunningham, as he was being driven to the station. It was the only remark he had made during the drive, but as Van Cheele had talked incessantly, his companion's silence had not been noticeable.

"A stray fox or two and some resident weasels. Nothing more formidable," said Van Cheele. The artist said nothing.

"What did you mean about a wild beast?" said Van Cheele later, when they were on the platform.

"Nothing. My imagination. Here is the train," said Cunningham.

That afternoon, Van Cheele went for one of his frequent rambles through his woodland property. He had a stuffed bittern in his study, and knew the names of quite a number of wild flowers, so his aunt had possibly some justification in describing him as a great naturalist. At any rate, he was a great walker. It was his custom to take mental notes of everything he saw during his walks, not so much for the purpose of assisting contemporary

science as to provide topics for conversation afterwards. When the bluebells began to show themselves in flower, he made a point of informing everyone of the fact; the season of the year might have warned his hearers of the likelihood of such an occurrence, but at least they felt that he was being absolutely frank with them.

What Van Cheele saw on this particular afternoon was, however, something far removed from his ordinary range of experience. On a shelf of smooth stone overhanging a deep pool in the hollow of an oak coppice, a boy of about sixteen lay asprawl, drying his wet brown limbs luxuriously in the sun. His wet hair, parted by a recent dive, lay close to his head, and his light-brown eyes, so light that there was an almost tigerish gleam in them, were turned towards Van Cheele with a certain lazy watchfulness. It was an unexpected apparition, and Van Cheele found himself engaged in the novel process of thinking before he spoke. Where on earth could this wild-looking boy hail from? The miller's wife had lost a child some two months ago, supposed to have been swept away by the mill race, but that had been a mere baby, not a half-grown lad.

"What are you doing there?" he demanded.

"Obviously, sunning myself," replied the boy.

"Where do you live?"

"Here, in these woods."

"You can't live in the woods," said Van Cheele.

"They are very nice woods," said the boy, with a touch of patronage in his voice.

"But where do you sleep at night?"

"I don't sleep at night: that's my busiest time."

Van Cheele began to have an irritated feeling that he was grappling with a problem that was eluding him.

"What do you feed on?" he asked.

"Flesh," said the boy, and he pronounced the word with slow relish, as though he were tasting it.

"Flesh! What flesh?"

"Since it interests you, rabbits, wild fowl, hares, poultry, lambs in their season, children when I can get any – they're usually too well locked in at night, when I do most of my hunting. It's quite two months since I tasted child flesh."

Ignoring the chaffing nature of the last remark, Van Cheele tried to draw the boy on the subject of possible poaching operations.

"You're talking rather through your hat when you speak of feeding on hares." Considering the nature of the boy's toilet, the simile was hardly an apt one. "Our hillside hares aren't easily caught."

"At night I hunt on four feet," was the somewhat cryptic response.

"I suppose you mean that you hunt with a dog?" hazarded Van Cheele.

The boy rolled slowly over onto his back and laughed a weird low laugh that was pleasantly like a chuckle and disagreeably like a snarl.

"I don't fancy any dog would be very anxious for my company, especially at night."

Van Cheele began to feel that there was something positively uncanny about the strange-eyed, strange-tongued youngster.

"I can't have you staying in these woods," he declared authoritatively.

"I fancy you'd rather have me here than in your house," said the boy.

The prospect of this wild, nude animal in Van Cheele's primly ordered house was certainly an alarming one.

"If you don't go, I shall have to make you," said Van Cheele.

The boy turned like a flash, plunged into the pool and in a moment had flung his wet and glistening body halfway up the bank where Van Cheele was standing. In an otter the movement would not have been remarkable; in a boy, Van Cheele found it sufficiently startling. His foot slipped as he made an involuntary backward movement, and he found himself almost prostrate on the slippery weed-grown bank, with those tigerish yellow eyes not very far from his own. Almost instinctively he half-raised his hand to his throat. The boy laughed again, a laugh in which the snarl had nearly driven out the chuckle, and then, with another of his astonishing lightning movements, plunged out of view into a yielding tangle of weed and fern.

"What an extraordinary wild animal!" said Van Cheele as he picked himself up. And then he recalled Cunningham's remark: "There is a wild beast in your woods."

Walking slowly homeward, Van Cheele began to turn over in his mind various local occurrences which might be traceable to the existence of this astonishing young savage.

Something had been thinning the game in the woods lately, poultry had been missing from the farms, hares were growing unaccountably scarcer, and complaints had reached him of lambs being carried off bodily from the hills. Was it possible that this wild boy was really hunting the countryside in company with some clever poacher dog? He had spoken of hunting "four-footed" by night – but then again, he had hinted strangely at no dog caring to come near him, "especially at night". It was certainly puzzling. And then, as Van Cheele ran his mind over the various depredations that had been committed during the last month or two, he came suddenly to a dead stop, alike in his walk and his speculations. The child missing from the mill two months ago – the accepted theory was that it had tumbled into the mill race and been swept away, but the mother had always declared she had heard a shriek on the hill side of the house, in the opposite direction from the water. It was unthinkable, of course, but he wished that the boy had not made that uncanny remark about child flesh eaten two months ago. Such dreadful things should not be said even in fun.

Van Cheele, contrary to his usual wont, did not feel disposed to be communicative about his discovery in the wood. His position as a parish councillor and justice of the peace seemed somehow compromised by the fact that he was harbouring a personality of such doubtful repute on his property: there was even a possibility that a heavy bill of damages for raided lambs and poultry might be laid at his door. At dinner that night he was quite unusually silent.

"Where's your voice gone to?" said his aunt. "One would think you had seen a wolf."

Van Cheele, who was not familiar with the old saying, thought the remark rather foolish: if he *had* seen a wolf on his property, his tongue would have been extraordinarily busy with the subject.

At breakfast next morning Van Cheele was conscious that his feeling of uneasiness regarding yesterday's episode had not wholly disappeared, and he resolved to go by train to the neighbouring cathedral town, hunt up Cunningham and learn from him what he had really seen that had prompted the remark about a wild beast in the woods. With this resolution taken, his usual cheerfulness partially returned, and he hummed a bright little melody as he sauntered to the morning room for his customary cigarette. As he entered the room, the melody made way abruptly for a pious invocation. Gracefully asprawl on the ottoman, in an attitude of almost exaggerated repose, was the boy of the woods. He was drier than when Van Cheele had last seen him, but no other alteration was noticeable in his toilet.

"How dare you come here?" asked Van Cheele furiously.

"You told me I was not to stay in the woods," said the boy calmly.

"But not to come here. Supposing my aunt should see you!"

And with a view to minimizing that catastrophe, Van Cheele hastily obscured as much of his unwelcome guest as possible under the folds of a *Morning Post*. At that moment his aunt entered the room.

"This is a poor boy who has lost his way – and lost his memory. He doesn't know who he is or where he comes from," explained Van Cheele desperately, glancing apprehensively at the waif's face to see whether he was going to add inconvenient candour to his other savage propensities.

Miss Van Cheele was enormously interested.

"Perhaps his underlinen is marked," she suggested.

"He seems to have lost most of that, too," said Van Cheele, making frantic little grabs at the *Morning Post* to keep it in its place.

A naked homeless child appealed to Miss Van Cheele as warmly as a stray kitten or derelict puppy would have done.

"We must do all we can for him," she decided, and in a very short time a messenger, dispatched to the rectory, where a page boy was kept, had returned with a suit of pantry clothes and the necessary accessories of shirt, shoes, collar, etc. Clothed, clean and groomed, the boy lost none of his uncanniness in Van Cheele's eyes, but his aunt found him sweet.

"We must call him something till we know who he really is," she said. "Gabriel-Ernest, I think: those are nice suitable names."

Van Cheele agreed, but he privately doubted whether they were being grafted onto a nice, suitable child. His misgivings were not diminished by the fact that his staid and elderly spaniel had bolted out of the house at the first incoming of the boy, and now obstinately remained shivering and yapping at the farther end of the orchard, while the canary, usually as vocally industrious as Van Cheele himself, had put itself on an allowance of frightened cheeps. More than ever he was resolved to consult Cunningham without loss of time.

As he drove off to the station, his aunt was arranging that Gabriel-Ernest should help her to entertain the infant members of her Sunday-school class at tea that afternoon.

Cunningham was not at first disposed to be communicative.

"My mother died of some brain trouble," he explained, "so you will understand why I am averse to dwelling on anything of an impossibly fantastic nature that I may see or think that I have seen."

"But what *did* you see?" persisted Van Cheele.

"What I thought I saw was something so extraordinary that no really sane man could dignify it with the credit of having actually happened. I was standing, the last evening I was with you, half-hidden in the hedge-growth by the orchard gate, watching the dying glow of the sunset. Suddenly I became aware of a naked boy, a bather from some neighbouring pool, I took him to be, who was standing out on the bare hillside also watching the sunset. His pose was so suggestive of some wild faun of Pagan myth that I instantly wanted to engage him as a model, and in another moment I think I should have hailed him. But just then the sun dipped out of view, and all the orange and pink slid out of the landscape, leaving it cold and grey. And at the same moment an astounding thing happened – the boy vanished too!"

"What! vanished away into nothing?" asked Van Cheele excitedly.

"No: that is the dreadful part of it," answered the artist. "On the open hillside where the boy had been standing a second ago, stood a large wolf, blackish in colour, with gleaming fangs and cruel, yellow eyes. You may think—"

But Van Cheele did not stop for anything as futile as thought. Already he was tearing at top speed towards the station. He dismissed the idea of a telegram. "Gabriel-Ernest is a werewolf" was a hopelessly inadequate effort at conveying the situation, and his aunt would think it was a code message to which he had omitted to give her the key. His one hope was that he might reach home before sundown. The cab which he chartered at the other end of the railway journey bore him with what seemed exasperating slowness along the country roads, which were pink and mauve with the flush of the sinking sun. His aunt was putting away some unfinished jams and cake when he arrived.

"Where is Gabriel-Ernest?" he almost screamed.

"He is taking the little Toop child home," said his aunt. "It was getting so late, I thought it wasn't safe to let it go back alone. What a lovely sunset, isn't it?"

But Van Cheele, although not oblivious of the glow in the western sky, did not stay to discuss its beauties. At a speed for which he was scarcely geared, he raced along the narrow lane that led to the home of the Toops. On one side ran the swift current of the mill stream, on the other rose the stretch of bare hillside. A dwindling rim of red sun showed still on the skyline, and the next turning must bring him in view of the ill-assorted couple he was pursuing. Then the colour went suddenly out of things, and a grey light settled itself with a quick shiver over the landscape. Van Cheele heard a shrill wail of fear and stopped running.

Nothing was ever seen again of the Toop child or Gabriel-Ernest, but the latter's discarded garments were found lying in the road, so it was assumed that the child had fallen into the water, and that the boy had stripped and jumped in, in a vain endeavour to save it. Van Cheele and some workmen who were nearby at the time testified to having heard a child scream loudly just near the spot where the clothes were found. Mrs Toop, who had eleven other children, was decently resigned to her bereavement, but Miss Van Cheele sincerely mourned her lost foundling. It was on her initiative that a memorial brass was put up in the parish church to "Gabriel-Ernest, an unknown boy, who bravely sacrificed his life for another".

Van Cheele gave way to his aunt in most things, but he flatly refused to subscribe to the Gabriel-Ernest memorial.

Sredni Vashtar

CONRADIN WAS ten years old, and the doctor had pronounced his professional opinion that the boy would not live another five years. The doctor was silky and effete, and counted for little, but his opinion was endorsed by Mrs De Ropp, who counted for nearly everything. Mrs De Ropp was Conradin's cousin and guardian, and in his eyes she represented those three fifths of the world that are necessary and disagreeable and real; the other two fifths, in perpetual antagonism to the foregoing, were summed up in himself and his imagination. One of these days Conradin supposed he would succumb to the mastering pressure of wearisome necessary things – such as illnesses and coddling restrictions and drawn-out dullness. Without his imagination, which was rampant under the spur of loneliness, he would have succumbed long ago.

Mrs De Ropp would never, in her honestest moments, have confessed to herself that she disliked Conradin, though she might have been dimly aware that thwarting him "for his good" was a duty which she did not find particularly irksome. Conradin hated her with a desperate sincerity which he was perfectly able to mask. Such few pleasures as he could contrive for himself gained an added relish from the likelihood that they would be displeasing to his guardian, and from the realm of his imagination she was locked out – an unclean thing, which should find no entrance.

In the dull, cheerless garden, overlooked by so many windows that were ready to open with a message not to do this or that, or a reminder that medicines were due, he found little attraction. The few fruit trees that it contained were set jealously apart from his plucking, as though they were rare specimens of their kind blooming in an arid waste: it would probably have been difficult to find a market gardener who would have offered ten shillings for their entire yearly produce. In a forgotten corner, however, almost hidden behind a dismal shrubbery, was a disused tool shed of respectable proportions, and within its walls Conradin found a haven, something that took on the varying aspects of a playroom and a cathedral. He had peopled it with a

legion of familiar phantoms, evoked partly from fragments of history and partly from his own brain, but it also boasted two inmates of flesh and blood. In one corner lived a ragged-plumaged Houdan hen, on which the boy lavished an affection that had scarcely another outlet. Further back in the gloom stood a large hutch, divided into two compartments, one of which was fronted with close iron bars. This was the abode of a large polecat-ferret, which a friendly butcher-boy had once smuggled, cage and all, into its present quarters, in exchange for a long-secreted hoard of small silver. Conradin was dreadfully afraid of the lithe, sharp-fanged beast, but it was his most treasured possession. Its very presence in the tool shed was a secret and fearful joy, to be kept scrupulously from the knowledge of the "Woman", as he privately dubbed his cousin. And one day, out of Heaven knows what material, he spun the beast a wonderful name, and from that moment it grew into a god and a religion. The Woman indulged in religion once a week at a church nearby, and took Conradin with her, but to him the church service was an alien rite in the House of Rimmon. Every Thursday, in the dim and musty silence of the tool shed, he worshipped with mystic and elaborate ceremonial before the wooden hutch where dwelt Sredni Vashtar, the great ferret. Red flowers in their season and scarlet berries in the wintertime were offered at his shrine, for he was a god who laid some special stress on the fierce impatient side of things, as opposed to the Woman's religion – which, as far as Conradin could observe, went to great lengths in the contrary direction. And on great festivals, powdered nutmeg was strewn in front

of his hutch, an important feature of the offering being that the nutmeg had to be stolen. These festivals were of irregular occurrence, and were chiefly appointed to celebrate some passing event. On one occasion, when Mrs De Ropp suffered from acute toothache for three days, Conradin kept up the festival during the entire three days, and almost succeeded in persuading himself that Sredni Vashtar was personally responsible for the toothache. If the malady had lasted for another day, the supply of nutmeg would have given out.

The Houdan hen was never drawn into the cult of Sredni Vashtar. Conradin had long ago settled that she was an Anabaptist. He did not pretend to have the remotest knowledge as to what an Anabaptist was, but he privately hoped that it was dashing and not very respectable. Mrs De Ropp was the ground plan on which he based and detested all respectability.

After a while, Conradin's absorption in the tool shed began to attract the notice of his guardian. "It is not good for him to be pottering down there in all weathers," she promptly decided, and at breakfast one morning she announced that the Houdan hen had been sold and taken away overnight. With her short-sighted eyes she peered at Conradin, waiting for an outbreak of rage and sorrow, which she was ready to rebuke with a flow of excellent precepts and reasoning. But Conradin said nothing: there was nothing to be said. Something perhaps in his white-set face gave her a momentary qualm, for at tea that afternoon there was toast on the table, a delicacy which she usually banned on the ground that it was bad for him – also because the making of it "gave trouble", a deadly offence in the middle-class feminine eye.

"I thought you liked toast," she exclaimed with an injured air, observing that he did not touch it.

"Sometimes," said Conradin.

In the shed that evening there was an innovation in the worship of the hutch-god. Conradin had been wont to chant his praises; tonight he asked a boon.

"Do one thing for me, Sredni Vashtar."

The thing was not specified. As Sredni Vashtar was a god, he must be supposed to know. And choking back a sob as he looked at that other empty corner, Conradin went back to the world he so hated.

And every night, in the welcome darkness of his bedroom, and every evening in the dusk of the tool shed, Conradin's bitter litany went up: "Do one thing for me, Sredni Vashtar."

Mrs De Ropp noticed that the visits to the shed did not cease, and one day she made a further journey of inspection.

"What are you keeping in that locked hutch?" she asked. "I believe it's guinea pigs. I'll have them all cleared away."

Conradin shut his lips tight, but the Woman ransacked his bedroom till she found the carefully hidden key, and forthwith marched down to the shed to complete her discovery. It was a cold afternoon, and Conradin had been bidden to keep to the house. From the farthest window of the dining room the door of the shed could just be seen beyond the corner of the shrubbery, and there Conradin stationed himself. He saw the Woman enter, and then he imagined her opening the door of the sacred hutch and peering down with her short-sighted eyes into the thick straw bed where his god lay hidden. Perhaps she would prod at the straw in her clumsy

impatience. And Conradin fervently breathed his prayer for the last time. But he knew as he prayed that he did not believe. He knew that the Woman would come out presently with that pursed smile he loathed so well on her face, and that in an hour or two the gardener would carry away his wonderful god – a god no longer, but a simple brown ferret in a hutch. And he knew that the Woman would triumph always as she triumphed now, and that he would grow ever more sickly under her pestering and domineering and superior wisdom, till one day nothing would matter much more with him, and the doctor would be proved right. And in the sting and misery of his defeat, he began to chant loudly and defiantly the hymn of his threatened idol:

Sredni Vashtar went forth,
His thoughts were red thoughts and his teeth
   were white.
His enemies called for peace, but he brought
   them death.
Sredni Vashtar the Beautiful.

And then of a sudden he stopped his chanting and drew closer to the window pane. The door of the shed still stood ajar as it had been left, and the minutes were slipping by. They were long minutes, but they slipped by nevertheless. He watched the starlings running and flying in little parties across the lawn; he counted them over and over again, with one eye always on that swinging door. A sour-faced maid came in to lay the table for tea, and still Conradin stood and waited and watched. Hope had crept by inches into his heart, and now a look of triumph began to blaze in his eyes that had only known the wistful patience of defeat. Under his breath, with a furtive exultation, he began once again the paean of victory and devastation. And presently his eyes were rewarded: out through that doorway came a long, low, yellow-and-brown beast, with eyes a-blink at the waning daylight and dark wet stains around the fur of jaws and throat. Conradin dropped on his knees. The great polecat-ferret made its way down to a small brook at the foot of the garden, drank for a moment, then crossed a little plank bridge and was lost to sight in the bushes. Such was the passing of Sredni Vashtar.

"Tea is ready," said the sour-faced maid. "Where is the mistress?"

"She went down to the shed some time ago," said Conradin.

And while the maid went to summon her mistress
to tea, Conradin fished a toasting fork out of the side-
board drawer and proceeded to toast himself a piece
of bread. And during the toasting of it and the butter-
ing of it with much butter and the slow enjoyment of
eating it, Conradin listened to the noises and silences
which fell in quick spasms beyond the dining-room
door. The loud foolish screaming of the maid, the

answering chorus of wondering ejaculations from the kitchen region, the scuttering footsteps and hurried embassies for outside help – and then, after a lull, the scared sobbings and the shuffling tread of those who bore a heavy burden into the house.

"Whoever will break it to the poor child? I couldn't for the life of me!" exclaimed a shrill voice. And while they debated the matter among themselves, Conradin made himself another piece of toast.

The Storyteller

I T WAS A HOT AFTERNOON, and the railway carriage was correspondingly sultry, and the next stop was at Templecombe, nearly an hour ahead. The occupants of the carriage were a small girl and a smaller girl and a small boy. An aunt belonging to the children occupied one corner seat, and the farther corner seat on the opposite side was occupied by a bachelor who was a stranger to their party, but the small girls and the small boy emphatically occupied the compartment. Both the aunt and the children were conversational in a limited, persistent way, reminding one of the attentions of a housefly that refuses to be discouraged. Most of the aunt's remarks seemed to begin with "Don't," and nearly all of the children's remarks began with "Why?" The bachelor said nothing out loud.

"Don't, Cyril, don't," exclaimed the aunt, as the small boy began smacking the cushions of the seat, producing a cloud of dust at each blow.

"Come and look out of the window," she added.

The child moved reluctantly to the window. "Why are those sheep being driven out of that field?" he asked.

"I expect they are being driven to another field where there is more grass," said the aunt weakly.

"But there is lots of grass in that field," protested the boy; "there's nothing else but grass there. Aunt, there's lots of grass in that field."

"Perhaps the grass in the other field is better," suggested the aunt fatuously.

"Why is it better?" came the swift, inevitable question.

"Oh, look at those cows!" exclaimed the aunt. Nearly every field along the line had contained cows or bullocks, but she spoke as though she were drawing attention to a rarity.

"Why is the grass in the other field better?" persisted Cyril.

The frown on the bachelor's face was deepening to a scowl. He was a hard, unsympathetic man, the aunt decided in her mind. She was utterly unable to come to any satisfactory decision about the grass in the other field.

The smaller girl created a diversion by beginning to recite 'On the Road to Mandalay'. She only knew the first line, but she put her limited knowledge to the fullest possible use. She repeated the line over and over again in a dreamy but resolute and very audible voice: it seemed to the bachelor as though someone had had a bet with her that she could not repeat the line aloud two thousand times without stopping. Whoever it was who had made the wager was likely to lose his bet.

"Come over here and listen to a story," said the aunt, when the bachelor had looked twice at her and once at the communication cord.

The children moved listlessly towards the aunt's end of the carriage. Evidently her reputation as a storyteller did not rank high in their estimation.

In a low, confidential voice, interrupted at frequent intervals by loud, petulant questionings from her listeners, she began an unenterprising and deplorably uninteresting story about a little girl who was good and made friends with everyone on account of her goodness, and was finally saved from a mad bull by a number of rescuers who admired her moral character.

"Wouldn't they have saved her if she hadn't been good?" demanded the bigger of the small girls. It was exactly the question that the bachelor had wanted to ask.

"Well, yes," admitted the aunt lamely, "but I don't think they would have run quite so fast to her help if they had not liked her so much."

"It's the stupidest story I've ever heard," said the bigger of the small girls, with immense conviction.

"I didn't listen after the first bit, it was so stupid," said Cyril.

The smaller girl made no actual comment on the story, but she had long ago recommenced a murmured repetition of her favourite line.

"You don't seem to be a success as a storyteller," said the bachelor suddenly from his corner.

The aunt bristled in instant defence at this unexpected attack.

"It's a very difficult thing to tell stories that children can both understand and appreciate," she said stiffly.

"I don't agree with you," said the bachelor.

"Perhaps *you* would like to tell them a story," was the aunt's retort.

"Tell us a story," demanded the bigger of the small girls.

"Once upon a time," began the bachelor, "there was a little girl called Bertha, who was extraordinarily good."

The children's momentarily aroused interest began at once to flicker: all stories seemed dreadfully alike, no matter who told them.

"She did all that she was told, she was always truth-ful, she kept her clothes clean, ate milk puddings as though they were jam tarts, learnt her lessons perfectly and was polite in her manners."

"Was she pretty?" asked the bigger of the small girls.

"Not as pretty as any of you," said the bachelor, "but she was horribly good."

There was a wave of reaction in favour of the story: the word horrible in connection with goodness was a novelty that commended itself. It seemed to introduce a ring of truth that was absent from the aunt's tales of infant life.

"She was so good," continued the bachelor, "that she won several medals for goodness, which she always wore, pinned onto her dress. There was a medal for obedience, another medal for punctuality and a third for good behaviour. They were large metal medals, and they clicked against one another as she walked. No other child in the town where she lived had as many as three medals, so everybody knew that she must be an extra-good child."

"Horribly good," quoted Cyril.

"Everybody talked about her goodness, and the Prince of the country got to hear about it, and he said that

as she was so very good she might be allowed once a week to walk in his park, which was just outside the town. It was a beautiful park, and no children were ever allowed in it, so it was a great honour for Bertha to be allowed to go there."

"Were there any sheep in the park?" demanded Cyril.

"No," said the bachelor, "there were no sheep."

"Why weren't there any sheep?" came the inevitable question arising out of that answer.

The aunt permitted herself a smile, which might almost have been described as a grin.

"There were no sheep in the park," said the bachelor, "because the Prince's mother had once had a dream that her son would either be killed by a sheep or else by a clock falling on him. For that reason the Prince never kept a sheep in his park or a clock in his palace."

The aunt suppressed a gasp of admiration.

"Was the Prince killed by a sheep or by a clock?" asked Cyril.

"He is still alive, so we can't tell whether the dream will come true," said the bachelor unconcernedly. "Anyway, there were no sheep in the park, but there were lots of little pigs running all over the place."

"What colour were they?"

"Black with white faces, white with black spots, black all over, grey with white patches, and some were white all over."

The storyteller paused to let a full idea of the park's treasures sink into the children's imaginations, then he resumed:

"Bertha was rather sorry to find that there were no flowers in the park. She had promised her aunts, with tears in her eyes, that she would not pick any of the

kind Prince's flowers, and she had meant to keep her promise, so of course it made her feel silly to find that there were no flowers to pick."

"Why weren't there any flowers?"

"Because the pigs had eaten them all," said the bachelor promptly. "The gardeners had told the Prince that you couldn't have pigs and flowers, so he decided to have pigs and no flowers."

There was a murmur of approval at the excellence of the Prince's decision: so many people would have decided the other way.

"There were lots of other delightful things in the park. There were ponds with gold and blue and green fish in them, and trees with beautiful parrots that said clever things at a moment's notice, and humming birds that hummed all the popular tunes of the day. Bertha walked up and down and enjoyed herself immensely, and thought to herself: 'If I were not so extraordinarily good, I should not have been allowed to come into this beautiful park and enjoy all that there is to be seen in it' – and her three medals clinked against one another as she walked and helped to remind her how very good she really was. Just then an enormous wolf came prowling into the park to see if it could catch a fat little pig for its supper."

"What colour was it?" asked the children, amid an immediate quickening of interest.

"Mud colour all over, with a black tongue and pale-grey eyes that gleamed with unspeakable ferocity. The first thing that it saw in the park was Bertha: her pinafore was so spotlessly white and clean that it could be seen from a great distance. Bertha saw the wolf and saw that it was stealing towards her, and she began to wish that she had never been allowed to come into the park. She ran as hard as she could, and the wolf came after her with huge leaps and bounds. She managed to reach a shrubbery of myrtle bushes and she hid herself in one of the thickest of the bushes. The wolf came sniffing among the branches, its black tongue lolling out of its mouth and its pale-grey eyes glaring with rage. Bertha was terribly frightened, and thought to herself: 'If I had not been so extraordinarily good I should have been safe in the town at this moment.' However, the scent of the myrtle was so strong that the wolf could not sniff out where Bertha was hiding, and the bushes were so thick that he might have hunted about in them for a long time without catching sight of her, so he thought he might as well go off and catch a little pig instead. Bertha was trembling very much at having the wolf prowling and sniffing so near her, and as she trembled, the medal for obedience clinked against the medals for good conduct and punctuality. The wolf was just moving away when he heard the sound of the medals clinking and stopped to listen: they clinked again in a bush quite near him. He dashed into the bush, his pale-grey eyes gleaming with ferocity and triumph, and dragged Bertha out and devoured her to the last morsel. All that was left of her were her shoes, bits of clothing and the three medals for goodness."

"Were any of the little pigs killed?"

"No, they all escaped."

"The story began badly," said the smaller of the small girls, "but it had a beautiful ending."

"It is the most beautiful story that I ever heard," said the bigger of the small girls, with immense decision.

"It is the *only* beautiful story I have ever heard," said Cyril.

A dissentient opinion came from the aunt.

"A most improper story to tell young children! You have undermined the effect of years of careful teaching."

"At any rate," said the bachelor, collecting his belongings preparatory to leaving the carriage, "I kept them quiet for ten minutes, which was more than you were able to do."

"Unhappy woman!" he observed to himself as he walked down the platform of Templecombe station.

"For the next six months or so those children will assail her in public with demands for an improper story!"

The She-Wolf

L EONARD BILSITER WAS ONE of those people who have failed to find this world attractive or interesting, and who have sought compensation in an "unseen world" of their own experience or imagination – or invention. Children do that sort of thing successfully, but children are content to convince themselves, and do not vulgarize their beliefs by trying to convince other people. Leonard Bilsiter's beliefs were for "the few" – that is to say, anyone who would listen to him.

His dabblings in the unseen might not have carried him beyond the customary platitudes of the drawing-room visionary if accident had not reinforced his stock-in-trade of mystical lore. In company with a friend, who was interested in a Ural mining concern, he had made a trip across Eastern Europe at a moment when the great Russian railway strike was developing from a threat to a reality: its outbreak caught him on the return journey, somewhere on the further side of

Perm, and it was while waiting for a couple of days at a wayside station in a state of suspended locomotion that he made the acquaintance of a dealer in harness and metalware, who profitably whiled away the tedium of the long halt by initiating his English travelling companion in a fragmentary system of folklore that he had picked up from Trans-Baikal traders and natives. Leonard returned to his home circle garrulous about his Russian strike experiences, but oppressively reticent about certain dark mysteries, which he alluded to under the resounding title of Siberian Magic. The reticence wore off in a week or two under the influence of an entire lack of general curiosity, and Leonard began to make more detailed allusions to the enormous powers which this new esoteric force – to use his own description of it – conferred on the initiated few who knew how to wield it. His aunt, Cecilia Hoops, who loved sensation perhaps rather better than she loved the truth, gave him as clamorous an advertisement as anyone could wish for by retailing an account of how he had turned a vegetable marrow into a wood pigeon before her very eyes. As a manifestation of the possession of supernatural powers, the story was discounted in some quarters by the respect accorded to Mrs Hoops's powers of imagination.

However divided opinion might be on the question of Leonard's status as a wonderworker or a charlatan, he certainly arrived at Mary Hampton's house party with a reputation for pre-eminence in one or other of those professions, and he was not disposed to shun such publicity as might fall to his share. Esoteric forces and unusual powers figured largely in whatever conversation he or his aunt had a share in, and his own performances, past and potential, were the subject of mysterious hints and dark avowals.

"I wish you would turn me into a wolf, Mr Bilsiter," said his hostess at luncheon the day after his arrival.

"My dear Mary," said Colonel Hampton, "I never knew you had a craving in that direction."

"A she-wolf, of course," continued Mrs. Hampton: it would be too confusing to change one's sex as well as one's species at a moment's notice."

"I don't think one should jest on these subjects," said Leonard.

"I'm not jesting, I'm quite serious, I assure you. Only don't do it today: we have only eight available bridge players, and it would break up one of our tables. Tomorrow we shall be a larger party. Tomorrow night, after dinner—"

"In our present imperfect understanding of these hidden forces, I think one should approach them with humbleness rather than mockery," observed Leonard, with such severity that the subject was forthwith dropped.

Clovis Sangrail had sat unusually silent during the discussion on the possibilities of Siberian Magic; after lunch he side-tracked Lord Pabham into the comparative seclusion of the billiard room and delivered himself of a searching question.

"Have you such a thing as a she-wolf in your collection of wild animals? A she-wolf of moderately good temper?"

Lord Pabham considered. "There is Louisa," he said, "a rather fine specimen of the timber-wolf. I got her two years ago in exchange for some Arctic foxes. Most of my animals get to be fairly tame before they've been with me very long; I think I can say Louisa has an angelic temper, as she-wolves go. Why do you ask?"

"I was wondering whether you would lend her to me for tomorrow night," said Clovis, with the careless solicitude of one who borrows a collar stud or a tennis racquet.

"Tomorrow night?"

"Yes, wolves are nocturnal animals, so the late hours won't hurt her," said Clovis, with the air of one who has taken everything into consideration. "One of your men could bring her over from Pabham Park after dusk, and with a little help he ought to be able to smuggle her into the conservatory at the same moment that Mary Hampton makes an unobtrusive exit."

Lord Pabham stared at Clovis for a moment in

pardonable bewilderment, then his face broke into a wrinkled network of laughter.

"Oh, that's your game, is it? You are going to do a little Siberian Magic on your own account. And is Mrs Hampton willing to be a fellow conspirator?"

"Mary is pledged to see me through with it, if you will guarantee Louisa's temper."

"I'll answer for Louisa," said Lord Pabham.

By the following day the house party had swollen to larger proportions, and Bilsiter's instinct for self-advertisement expanded duly under the stimulant of an increased audience. At dinner that evening he held forth at length on the subject of unseen forces and untested powers, and his flow of impressive eloquence continued unabated while coffee was being served in the drawing room preparatory to a general migration to the card room.

His aunt ensured a respectful hearing for his utterances, but her sensation-loving soul hankered after something more dramatic than mere vocal demonstration.

"Won't you do something to convince them of your powers, Leonard?" she pleaded. "Change something into another shape. He can, you know, if he only chooses to," she informed the company.

"Oh, do," said Mavis Pellington earnestly, and her request was echoed by nearly everyone present. Even those who were not open to conviction were perfectly willing to be entertained by an exhibition of amateur conjuring.

Leonard felt that something tangible was expected of him.

"Has anyone present," he asked, "got a three-penny bit or some small object of no particular value?"

"You're surely not going to make coins disappear, or something primitive of that sort?" said Clovis contemptuously.

"I think it very unkind of you not to carry out my suggestion of turning me into a wolf," said Mary Hampton, as she crossed over to the conservatory to give her macaws their usual tribute from the dessert dishes.

"I have already warned you of the danger of treating these powers in a mocking spirit," said Leonard solemnly.

"I don't believe you can do it," laughed Mary provocatively from the conservatory. "I dare you to do it if you can. I defy you to turn me into a wolf."

As she said this she was lost to view behind a clump of azaleas.

"Mrs Hampton—" began Leonard with increased solemnity, but he got no further. A breath of chill air seemed to rush across the room, and at the same time the macaws broke forth into ear-splitting screams.

"What on earth is the matter with those confounded birds, Mary?" exclaimed Colonel Hampton; at the same moment an even more piercing scream from Mavis Pellington stampeded the entire company from their seats. In various attitudes of helpless horror or instinctive defence, they confronted the evil-looking grey beast that was peering at them from amid a setting of fern and azalea.

Mrs Hoops was the first to recover from the general chaos of fright and bewilderment.

"Leonard!" she screamed shrilly to her nephew, "turn it back into Mrs Hampton at once! It may fly at us at any moment. Turn it back!"

"I – I don't know how to," faltered Leonard, who looked more scared and horrified than anyone.

"What!" shouted Colonel Hampton, "you've taken the abominable liberty of turning my wife into a wolf, and now you stand there calmly and say you can't turn her back again!"

To do strict justice to Leonard, calmness was not a distinguishing feature of his attitude at the moment.

"I assure you I didn't turn Mrs Hampton into a wolf: nothing was farther from my intentions," he protested.

"Then where is she, and how came that animal into the conservatory?" demanded the Colonel.

"Of course we must accept your assurance that you didn't turn Mrs Hampton into a wolf," said Clovis politely, "but you will agree that appearances are against you."

"Are we to have all these recriminations with that beast standing there ready to tear us to pieces?" wailed Mavis indignantly.

"Lord Pabham, you know a good deal about wild beasts—" suggested Colonel Hampton.

"The wild beasts that I have been accustomed to," said Lord Pabham, "have come with proper credentials from well-known dealers, or have been bred in my own menagerie. I've never before been confronted with an animal that walks unconcernedly out of an azalea bush, leaving a charming and popular hostess unaccounted for. As far as one can judge from outward characteristics," he continued, "it has the appearance of a well-grown female of the North American timber-wolf, a variety of the common species *canis lupus*."

"Oh, never mind its Latin name," screamed Mavis, as the beast came a step or two further into the room. "Can't you entice it away with food and shut it up where it can't do any harm?"

"If it is really Mrs Hampton, who has just had a very good dinner, I don't suppose food will appeal to it very strongly," said Clovis.

"Leonard," beseeched Mrs Hoops tearfully, "even if this is none of your doing, can't you use your great powers to turn this dreadful beast into something harmless before it bites us all – a rabbit or something?"

"I don't suppose Colonel Hampton would care to have his wife turned into a succession of fancy animals as though we were playing a round game with her," interposed Clovis.

"I absolutely forbid it," thundered the Colonel.

"Most wolves that I've had anything to do with have been inordinately fond of sugar," said Lord Pabham. "If you like I'll try the effect on this one."

He took a piece of sugar from the saucer of his coffee cup and flung it to the expectant Louisa, who snapped it in mid-air. There was a sigh of relief from the company: a wolf that ate sugar when it might at the least have been employed in tearing macaws to pieces had already shed some of its terrors. The sigh deepened to a gasp of thanksgiving when Lord Pabham decoyed the animal out of the room by a pretended largesse of further sugar. There was an instant rush to the vacated conservatory. There was no trace of Mrs Hampton except the plate containing the macaws' supper.

"The door is locked on the inside!" exclaimed Clovis, who had deftly turned the key as he affected to test it.

Everyone turned towards Bilsiter.

"If you haven't turned my wife into a wolf," said Colonel Hampton, "will you kindly explain where she has disappeared to, since she obviously could not have gone through a locked door? I will not press you for an explanation of how a North American timber-wolf suddenly appeared in the conservatory, but I think I have some right to enquire what has become of Mrs Hampton."

Bilsiter's reiterated disclaimer was met with a general murmur of impatient disbelief.

"I refuse to stay another hour under this roof," declared Mavis Pellington.

"If our hostess has really vanished out of human form," said Mrs Hoops, "none of the ladies of the party can very well remain. I absolutely decline to be chaperoned by a wolf!"

"It's a she-wolf," said Clovis soothingly.

The correct etiquette to be observed under the unusual circumstances received no further elucidation. The sudden entry of Mary Hampton deprived the discussion of its immediate interest.

"Someone has mesmerized me," she exclaimed crossly. "I found myself in the game larder, of all places, being fed with sugar by Lord Pabham. I hate being mesmerized, and the doctor has forbidden me to touch sugar."

The situation was explained to her, as far as it permitted of anything that could be called explanation.

"Then you really did turn me into a wolf, Mr Bilsiter?" she exclaimed excitedly.

But Leonard had burned the boat in which he might now have embarked on a sea of glory. He could only shake his head feebly.

"It was I who took that liberty," said Clovis. "You see, I happen to have lived for a couple of years in North-Eastern Russia, and I have more than a tourist's acquaintance with the magic craft of that region. One does not care to speak about these strange powers, but once in a way, when one hears a lot of nonsense being talked about them, one is tempted to show what Siberian magic can accomplish in the hands of someone who really understands it. I yielded to that temptation. May I have some brandy? The effort has left me rather faint."

If Leonard Bilsiter could at that moment have transformed Clovis into a cockroach and then have stepped on him he would gladly have performed both operations.

Extra Material
for Younger Readers

THE WRITER

Hector Hugh Munro ("Saki" was his writing name) was the third child of a British upper-middle-class family. Hector was born in 1870 in Burma, now known as Myanmar, which at that time was part of the British Raj. His Scottish father, Charles Augustus Munro, was Inspector General of the Indian Imperial Police. His mother, Mary Frances Mercer, was the daughter of a Rear Admiral. Tragically she died when Hector was only two, during a visit to England, so Hector never got to know her. He was brought up by his strict and religious grandmother and aunts in a village near Barnstaple in Devon – their repressive child-rearing techniques are evident in the way that many of his stories feature unpleasant aunts – and educated first at home with governesses and then at Bedford School.

Later in his childhood his father, having retired, took him and his siblings on extended tours of Europe to further their education.

In his early twenties Hector followed his father's footsteps by joining the police service in Burma, but after a year he had to abandon this career when he contracted malaria. Back in England, he started writing for newspapers and magazines. His way of writing – sarcastic, observational – was well received by readers. Particularly successful were his 'Alice in Westminster' pieces for the *Westminster Gazette,* in which he re-imagined Lewis Carrol's little girl Alice from *Alice in Wonderland* as a character trying to make sense of the political goings-on in the houses of parliament. In 1902 these pieces were collected together in a book called *The Westminster Alice,* and the book was so success-ful that Hector – or Saki – became a famous writer. Two years later *Reginald,* his first collection of short stories, was published.

Most commentators believe that Hector took the "Saki" pen name from one of two possible sources: *The Rubáiyát of Omar Khayyám* – a translation into

English by Edward FitzGerald of about 1,000 Persian poems attributed to the Persian mathematician, philosopher and poet Omar Khayyám (1048–1131) – in which the cupbearer to the gods is called Saki; or from a monkey in South America also known as a saki.

Hector worked as the foreign correspondent of the Morning Post until his father's death in 1908, when he retired and moved to France to be Saki, the writer, full-time. His stories were hugely popular, and were collected into book form in 1910 (*Reginald in Russia*) and 1911 (*The Chronicles of Clovis*). He also wrote two novels in this period, but he remains better known for his short stories. In 1914 he published *Beasts and Super-Beasts*, which along with *The Chronicles of Clovis* represents his finest work.

When the First World War broke out in 1914, Hector was too old to enlist, but somehow he managed to volunteer as an ordinary soldier in the Royal Fusiliers – he refused a commission as an officer. In November 1916 he was killed by a sniper's bullet in France. After his death, his sister Ethel is believed to have destroyed his private papers.

Two further collections of his work were published – he had managed to write some stories even in the trenches – and in the 1920s he was "rediscovered" as an important contributor to the short-story form.

THE BOOK

The stories in this book are taken from the several collections of short stories that Saki published. One ('Gabriel-Ernest') is taken from his second collection, *Reginald in Russia*, and two are taken from his third collection, *The Chronicles of Clovis* ('Sredni Vashtar', 'The Chaplet'). The majority, however, are taken from the book that sealed his reputation as a master of the form, *Beasts and Super-Beasts*. These are 'The She-Wolf', 'The Boar-Pig', 'The Open Window', 'The Schartz-Metterklume Method', 'The Storyteller' and 'The Lumber Room'. The title *Beasts and Super-Beasts* is a parody of *Man and Superman*, a play by George Bernard Shaw.

THE CHARACTERS

The Open Window

Framton Nuttel

Mr Nuttel is a highly strung man with nervous complaints: he is something of a hypochondriac, and has travelled to a peaceful location in order to take the "rest-cure" prescribed by his doctors. His sister has given him letters of introduction to several people in the area, and he is visiting the house of Mrs Sappleton.

The Niece

Vera Sappleton, a fifteen-year-old girl, is the niece of Mrs Sappleton. She has a very mature air for her age. She takes a quiet satisfaction in controlling the conversation with Mr Nuttel and exciting his nerves with an alarming and untrue tale about the tragic death of Mrs Sappleton's husband and children.

Mrs Sappleton

The aunt, Mrs Sappleton, is a devoted wife and mother who thinks about her family and its doings as much as Mr Nuttel thinks about his nerves and the suffering they cause him. When her "dead" husband and sons return home after a shooting trip, she is amazed to see Mr Nuttel flee in terror…

The Boar-Pig

Mrs Philidore Stossen

Mrs Stossen is a middle-aged lady of high self-regard who is very peeved that she and her daughter haven't been invited to the most important garden party of the season, organized by Mrs Cuvering, where "the Princess" will be in attendance. Dressed in fine clothes, she attempts to gatecrash the party by leading her daughter through the fruit garden and other difficult terrain.

Miss Matilda Cuvering

Matilda is the wildly mischievous thirteen-year-old daughter of Mrs Cuvering. Her bad behaviour

– force-feeding raspberry trifle down the throat of her saintly young cousin Claude so that no one can praise him for never having eaten too much dessert – has seen her banished from the party. She secretly unleashes the pig from the sty to prevent the two women from escaping home, and extracts a huge bribe from Mrs Stossen to resolve the situation.

Tarquin Superbus
A huge white Yorkshire boar-pig, and a "villainous-looking animal" according to Mrs Stossen.

The Chaplet

Clovis
Clovis Sangrail is a character who often occurs in Saki's stories, especially in Saki's third collection, *The Chronicles of Clovis*. He is the narrator of the story, so we don't learn much about him directly, but indirectly we can see that he enjoys mischief and is rather sly.

Monsieur Aristide Saucourt

Once the chef of the Grand Sybaris Hotel, Monsieur Saucourt is a culinary artiste of high renown and haughty pride. He has spent months perfecting a new signature dish, *Canetons à la mode d'Amblève*, and is presenting it for the first time in the restaurant of the hotel. When the diners don't pay much attention to the perfection he has created for them, instead applauding the musicians for playing a tune called 'The Chaplet', he breaks into a violent rage and plunges the orchestra leader's head into a tureen of soup.

The Lumber Room

Nicholas

Nicholas is a boy who insists there is a frog in his bread-and-milk even when told that such a thing is impossible – but he knows there is, because he put it there. It is this kind of impeccable logic that allows him to run rings around his aunt when she tries to punish him by organizing a beach trip for the other children and banning him from the gooseberry garden. By taking his aunt's words at face value, he manages to make her the victim of the punishment, rather than him.

Aunt

Aunt is a lady whose efforts to control and admonish the children are sneaky, leaving too many gaps in fact and logic, so she is easily tricked by Nicholas. For example, she has reproached him in the past for yielding when he hears the voice of the devil tempting him to do wrong things; so when she is trapped in the water tank and tells him to come into the forbidden gooseberry garden to help her, he answers that he cannot yield to the voice of the "Evil One".

The Schartz-Metterklume Method

Lady Carlotta

Lady Carlotta is an eccentric member of the upper classes who is mistaken for a governess, a certain Miss Hope. She takes up her duties within an unsuspecting family, intimidating the parents with her superior knowledge of wine and her claims to teach history by the Schartz-Metterklume Method. Her employment lasts one day, when she is found conducting the children in a physical enactment of a very unsuitable historical episode from Roman history.

Mrs Quabarl

The accidental employer of "Miss Hope" for one day, Mrs Quabarl is a very conventional woman who finds she cannot hold her own against the superior social confidence of her unusual new governess, and who is scandalized by the Schartz-Metterklume Method, which seems to involve her sons forcibly kidnapping the lodge-keeper's children.

Gabriel-Ernest

Van Cheele

Van Cheele is a member of the gentry who takes great pleasure in his woodland, but who one day finds a wild, naked boy in there – a boy who claims that he lives off "flesh". The boy later turns up in the house, where despite Van Cheele's misgivings – in the past few months poultry and lambs have gone missing, and a local child has disappeared – his aunt takes him in as foundling. Van Cheele tries to investigate, but by the time he realizes that the boy is a werewolf, it's too late…

Gabriel-Ernest

This is the name that Van Cheele's aunt gives to the boy when he appears in the house. The boy is wild in looks but speaks well and cunningly. Only later, after he has been entrusted with the company of other children, it is discovered that his wild ways in the woods are explained by his being a werewolf.

Cunningham

Cunningham is an artist and a recent visitor to Van Cheele's house who saw the boy turn into a wolf-like beast.

Aunt

Van Cheele's aunt is a naive and pleasant woman who is keen to mother the strange foundling; she never finds out that the boy is a werewolf, and after he and a child he was accompanying have disappeared, she even funds a plaque to be erected in memory of his name.

Sredni Vashtar

Conradin

Conradin is a sickly, lonely boy who is looked after by his cold and uncaring cousin. He isn't permitted much freedom or pleasure, but he secretly keeps a hen and a ferret in a shed at the bottom of the garden, and these companions help him to bear his unhappiness and his neglect, becoming part of a personal pagan religion. When his cousin finds the hen and takes it away, he prays to the ferret, which he calls Sredni Vashtar, to help him.

Mrs De Ropp

The cheerless and hypocritically religious cousin and guardian of Conradin, Mrs De Ropp is systematically killing Conradin's spirit with her mean-minded care. She becomes aware that the shed is providing him with some kind of pleasure and sustenance; she succeeds in taking the hen away, but the ferret – the great Sredni

Vashtar – perhaps responding to Conradin's worship and prayers, kills her.

The Storyteller

The Aunt

With four bored children to look after, little imagination and an unwavering focus on goodness, the aunt is ill-equipped to entertain her charges for a long train journey. She is aware that her fellow passenger is irritated by the children's querulous demands, and is worn out and exasperated by the children disliking the story she tells them, whose moral value is beyond dispute.

The Bachelor

Trying to read his newspaper in peace, driven mad by the bored children and the worthy aunt, the bachelor criticizes the aunt's dreary story, and takes up her challenge to tell a story of his own. In his story, an extraordinarily good little girl is eaten by a wolf, despite being so good, to the enormous appreciation of the listening children.

The She-Wolf

Leonard Bilsiter

A rather vain and unremarkable man, Leonard tries to gain admiration and regard by claiming he has mysterious magical powers, and responds to mockery – "I do wish you would turn me into a wolf", says his house party host Mrs Hampton – with humourless superiority. When he is tricked so that Mrs Hampton does appear to have turned into a wolf, his confidence crumbles: he denies that he has performed the task, and he confesses that he lacks the power.

Clovis Sangrail

Clovis also appears in 'The Chaplet', earlier in this collection. He is a charming and rather sly young man, prone to mischief. Bored and contemptuous of Leonard Bilsiter's claims to dabble in dark forces, he conspires with the host of the house party, Mrs Hampton, to play a monstrous trick. He borrows a tame she-wolf from a friend who has a collection of animals, and at an appropriate point in the conversation about Bilsiter's claims, Mrs Hampton duly vanishes, replaced by the wolf, to Bilsiter's horror.

MASTERS OF THE SHORT STORY

Saki, most of whose work was in the short-story form, might have been less highly regarded had he been around now, because the short story is much less popular than it used to be. These days, novels get all the attention. This is a shame, because the short story presents different challenges and opportunities to the longer novel form, and can be just as satisfying. In the period 1850 to 1950 there are dozens of masters of the short story. Here are a few who stand out.

O. Henry

An American writer born in North Carolina, "O. Henry" was the pen name of William Sydney Porter (1862–1910) – he started using this pen name when in prison for embezzlement. His stories are marked by wit and clever twists, especially their endings, and by warm characterization. His most famous short story is 'The Gift of the Magi', about a young married couple who want to buy each other Christmas presents but don't have enough money. O. Henry was a heavy drinker who died before reaching fifty because of his alcoholism.

Guy de Maupassant

Born in France in 1850, and dying just aged forty-three in an asylum, Maupassant is one of the finest European short-story writers, better known for his 300 stories than for his six novels. His work was influenced by the novelist Gustave Flaubert. Many of his stories are set in the Franco-Prussian war that took place in the years 1870 and 1871 – a war in which Maupassant was a volunteer – and deal with the way innocent civilians have their lives changed for ever by war. His story 'Boule de Suif' ('Butterball') – the first story he published and often considered his finest – is one of his Franco-Prussian stories.

Anton Chekhov

A doctor and playwright as well as a short-story writer, Anton Chekhov (1860–1904) was born in Russia. He initially wrote humorous pieces for newspapers and magazines to earn money. But as he wrote more, he became interested in the short story as a powerful literary form. By the time of his death from tuberculosis in 1904, Chekhov had written enough stories to fill ten large volumes. Some of these are among the most celebrated in the short-story genre.

TEST YOURSELF

Writers of short stories have a sharp eye for the telling detail and quirky observational powers. Did you read *Gabriel-Ernest and Other Tales* with close attention? Try this quiz to find out. The answers are overleaf.

1. In 'The Open Window', when the supposedly dead father and sons turn up to terrify Mr Nuttel, what does the youngest son sing to his little brown spaniel?
   A) 'Gertie, what a good hound'
   B) 'Bertie, now that you're found'
   C) 'Bertie, why do you bound?'
   D) 'Gertie, will you come round?'

2. In 'The Boar-Pig', what kind of pig is Tarquin Superbus?
   A) A huge white Yorkshire boar-pig
   B) A huge black Yorkshire boar-pig
   C) A huge short-legged Yorkshire boar-pig
   D) A huge Yorkshire pudding boar-pig

3. At the beginning of 'The Chaplet', what tune is the orchestra playing in the Amethyst dining hall of the Grand Sybaris Hotel?
   A) The 'Candy Floss Waiter' waltz
   B) The 'Sweet Candy Showgirl' waltz
   C) The 'Yorkshire Pudding Miner' waltz
   D) The 'Ice Cream Sailor' waltz

4. In 'The Lumber Room', Aunt gets trapped in something when she goes to the gooseberry garden. What does she get trapped in?
   A) A water tank
   B) A pond
   C) A potting shed
   D) A compromising situation

5. In 'The Schartz-Metterklume Method', how does Lady Carlotta, impersonating the governess Miss Hope, describe the Schartz-Metterklume method of teaching children history?
- A) Making children understand history by giving them a number-nine spanking with one of father's fives-bats
- B) Making children understand history by insisting on teaching it in French and Russian
- C) Making children understand history by acting it themselves
- D) Making children understand history by introducing them to the life stories of men and women who really lived

6. In 'Sredni Vashtar', what kind of hen does the lonely and poorly boy Conradin lavish much affection on?
- A) A rugged-plum Honduran Hen
- B) A ragged-plumaged Houdan Hen
- C) A regular-plumed Houdini Hen
- D) A Roger-Plumstone Handy Hen

7. In 'The Storyteller', what is the first line of the story told to the bored children by the bachelor?
- A) "Once upon a time, there was a little girl called Roberta, who always ate her milk puddings."
- B) "Once upon a time, there was a little girl called Gertie, who was exceptionally stupid."
- C) "Once upon a time, there was a little girl called Martha, who was eaten by a wolf."
- D) "Once upon a time, there was a little girl called Bertha, who was extraordinarily good."

8. In 'The She-Wolf', what kind of wolf does Clovis Sangrail borrow from the animal collector Lord Pabham in order to expose Leonard Bilsiter as a fraud?
- A) A North-American timber wolf
- B) A North-Armenian lumber wolf
- C) A North-Siberian fender wolf
- D) A North-Yorkshire pudding wolf.

ANSWERS

1–C
2–A
3–D
4–A
5–C
6–B
7–D
8–A

SCORES

1 to 3 correct: Are these short stories too long for you? **4 to 6 correct:** Not bad but the Schartz-Metterklume Method would improve your results. **7 to 8 correct:** You are a Master of the Short Story!